Oatmeal Is Not for Mustaches

by Thomas Rockwell

illustrated by Eileen Christelow

Holt, Rinehart and Winston · *New York*

Text copyright © 1984 by Thomas Rockwell
Illustrations copyright © 1984 by Eileen Christelow
All rights reserved, including the right to reproduce
this book or portions thereof in any form.
Published by Holt, Rinehart and Winston,
383 Madison Avenue, New York, New York 10017.
Published simultaneously in Canada by Holt, Rinehart
and Winston of Canada, Limited.

Library of Congress Cataloging in Publication Data
Rockwell, Thomas, 1933–
Oatmeal is not for mustaches.
Summary: Describes, in text and illustrations,
some of the usual and unusual uses for a variety of
familiar things.
1. Children's stories, American. I. Christelow, Eileen, ill. II. Title.
PZ7.R5949Oat 1984   [E]   84-9081
ISBN 0-03-063653-1

First Edition

Printed in the United States of America

1 3 5 7 9 10 8 6 4 2

ISBN 0-03-063653-1

Oatmeal Is Not for Mustaches

Morning is for waking up
to find that everything
is where it always is—
        sunlight in flouncy curtains,
        Mommy calling.

Morning is for backwards shirts,
inside-out pants,
a leg shirt!
arm pants,

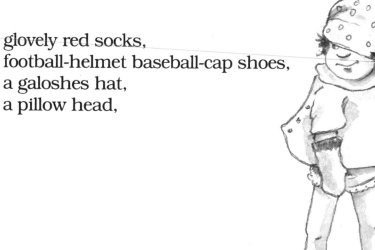

glovely red socks,
football-helmet baseball-cap shoes,
a galoshes hat,
a pillow head,

and
going
downstairs
carefully
backwards.

Mommy is for straightening everything out
without tickling too much.

A pot is for cooking,

carrying things,

a hat,

and drumming.

Oatmeal is for making mountains, lakes, and rivers in.

Oatmeal is for eating,
    and eating,
    and eating,

eating upside down from the top of the spoon,
eating right-side up from the bottom of the spoon,
    and eating,
    and eating,

(oatmeal is not for mustaches)

and eating,
and eating,
and eating,

and *finishing!*

A pot is for scrubbing.

A screen door is for giving yourself
chicken pox on your nose.

A puddle is for poking,
          wading,
          leaf boats,
          damming,

To be lifted up into a truck is scary.

But then inside it's like a little house:
strange clocks and shiny machinery, dangling dolls
and bears, pictures of ladies all over the ceiling.

Sometimes a truck is too big to SEE!

And then a sooty-greasy maybe-ogre climbs down
and asks Mommy questions to where.

careful splashing,

marching!

JUMPING!

A puddle is not for sitting.

The back of a truck is so big and dark . . .
it could be for
      an ogre's cave,
      shrinking smaller
      and smaller.

The screen door and the kitchen door
are for squeezing closed
while standing between . . .
like happy sandwiches.

A face is for making sad   growly   beautiful   squash
scary   painted   fish   angry   turtle   octopus   faces.

Breadsticks are cigars,

fangs,

fire-breathing-dragon nose fire,
fire-breathing-dragon ear,
nose, and fang fire,

and *breadsticks*, not toys.

I can suck spaghetti
because my name's not Freddie!

Rest time is for making blanket houses
—without chairs—

for building roads through bedspread hills,
with knuckle-bulldozers and finger-grubbers,
for flat-hand racing cars
—on separate beds—

for looking at books
for dreaming on mountaintops

or a sleeping giantess.

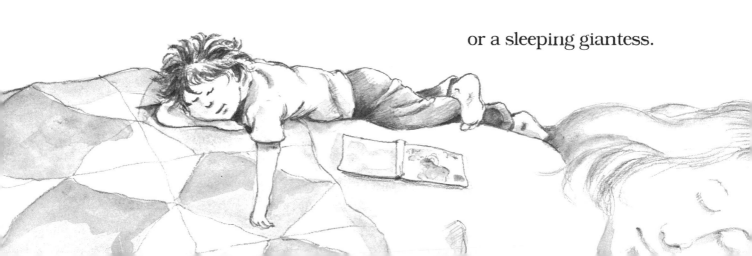

A closet is for hiding in
while Mommy calls
and pokes her broom
among the shadowy coats
and shoes.

The silence and the dimness in a closet
are for wondering in:
  where did Mommy go?

Overcoats are for
surprising Daddy from
when he comes home.

Grocery bags are for celery, onions, soap,
interesting sponges, *cookies!*
oatmeal, cheese, cans, boxes,
rolling oranges,

and a *kitten!*

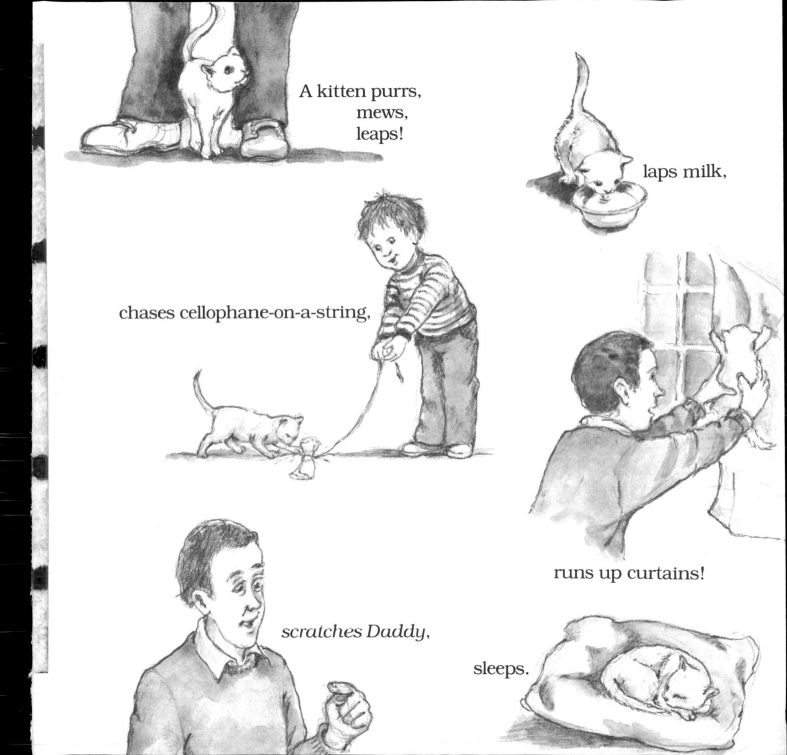

A kitten purrs,
mews,
leaps!

laps milk,

chases cellophane-on-a-string,

runs up curtains!

scratches Daddy,

sleeps.

Kittens are not for tables, kittens are for floors.
Or a chair.

Dinner is sometimes for spinach.

Spinach is for hiding.

Ketchup is for mustaches.

Plates are for parades.

Ice cream dishes are not for hats.

Night is for knots
and getting stuck in shirts,

Daddy bringing drinks of water,
Mommy showing that the shadowy
!?!THING!?!
is really just a chair with
clothes on it.

Night is for gazing at
the ceiling and the floor.

Night is for morning.